THE TISWAS BOOK OF SILLY SUPERSTITIONS

Hello there! This is the Tiswas team and we've been dipping into the nutty world of superstitious belief to bring you a selection of the zaniest superstitions imaginable!

For instance, did you know that if you wash the wrong part of your body first, put your clothes on in the wrong order, then eat the wrong food and with the wrong piece of cutlery you'll have such a lot of bad luck in store that you might as well go back to bed for the rest of the day? And that's before you set foot outside—which had better be the right one!

They're hilarious, ridiculous and totally silly—but we daren't fling a flan without them and we're sure you won't either!

So, read on with an open mind and a few wheelbarrows of cow dung scattered round the house—GOOD LUCK!!

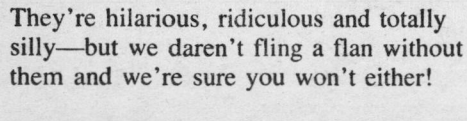

THE TISWAS BOOK OF SILLY SUPERSTITIONS

A CAROUSEL BOOK   0   552   54185   0

First published in Great Britain

PRINTING HISTORY
Carousel edition published 1981
Carousel edition reprinted 1981

Copyright © ATV Network Limited 1981
Compilation © Helen Piddock 1981
Illustrations copyright © Transworld Publishers Ltd. 1981

Carousel Books are published by
Transworld Publishers Ltd.,
Century House, 61–63 Uxbridge Road,
Ealing, London W5 5SA.

Printed and bound in Great Britain by
Cox & Wyman Ltd, Reading

THE TISWAS BOOK OF SILLY SUPERSTITIONS

Compiled by Helen Piddock
Illustrated by Bobbie Craig

Carousel Books

SILLY CONTENTS

THE TISWAS TEAM'S OWN SILLY SUPERSTITIONS!

CHRIS TARRANT'S favourite hobby is fishing. Many years ago he landed such an enormous fish, the catch went down in the record books. At the time he was wearing an old coat! Now, the coat is even older and falling apart at the seams, but Chris refuses to go fishing without it—he believes it brings him luck!

SALLY JAMES fervently believes in the saying **"help someone to salt and you'll help them to sorrow"**! She also doesn't like passing anyone on the stairs! (You'll find the origin of that superstition later in the book.)

BOB CAROLGEES will never whistle or wear anything green inside a theatre!

SPIT THE DOG believes it would be very unlucky to spit on a member of the Royal Family!

COF THE CAT tries not to sit in the warm on Friday 13th in case his cof gets better!

CHARLIE THE MONKEY, whenever he's in Wigan avoids standing under the palm trees in case a coconut falls on his head!

PC PLOD thinks it's unlucky to turn his truncheon over in his pocket!

ALBERT GRUMBLE believes it's unlucky to do any floor sweeping when there's a full moon!

ON STRIKE

THE PHANTOM FLAN FLING-ER believes that if he wears any colour apart from black his custard pies will lose their power!

RAZZ always eats his bread and condensed milk sandwiches on the first Thursday after the last Saturday before the 4th Wednesday after the 3rd Tuesday before the 2nd Sunday after the 5th Monday before Friday 13th—it tastes better!

NOW READ ON

FAMOUS PEOPLE'S SILLY SUPERSTITIONS!

Prince Philip always taps his polo helmet seven times for good luck before starting each game!

William Shakespeare believed that sleeping in a four hundred year old bed was the reason for his success as a writer!

Dr. Samuel Johnson always touched every wooden post that he passed and never stepped on the cracks between paving stones!

Queen Elizabeth II gave a coin in return for a present of cutlery as she believes that a friendship will be cut if you don't give something to someone who gives you a knife!

Winston Churchill had a lucky walking stick which he always took with him, particularly if he had to go anywhere on a Friday!

The American rocket **Vanguard 3** carried a St Christopher medallion for safety!

Tony Curtis believes it's very unlucky for a white cat to cross his path!

Diana Dors relies on a string of pearls for giving her good luck!

Sean Connery's lucky number is 17 and when he uses it during gambling he usually wins!

EVERY HOME SHOULD HAVE ONE!

If you get home one day and find that you can't get in, there's a very special routine you should follow to avoid bad luck! Once you've climbed through a conveniently open window you must go and open the front door. But **before you do anything else** you must climb back out through the window, then enter the front door in the usual way!

When you leave home you shouldn't look back at the house because it might cause bad luck for your journey!

In Virginia in the United States, it's believed that if you knock on someone's front door and there's no answer, it's a sign of death! (Far more likely there's no-one in!)

Next time you move to a new house, as soon as you arrive you must walk into every room carrying a loaf of bread and a plate of salt! The removal men may think you've gone a bit potty, but what you're doing is showing any spirits who might be lurking in the empty rooms that you mean them no harm. They in turn won't bother you for as long as you live there.

If you go out and find you've left something behind, you really ought to forget about it and carry on your way. But if it's vital to go back home and get it, when you arrive at home you must sit down and count to ten before setting off again!

It's bad luck to open the front door when the back door is already open, and also you shouldn't leave a house with all the doors open inside and out! This comes from the old Roman belief that evil spirits will easily be able to get inside. (If another word for an "evil spirit" is a "burglar", then this isn't surprising!)

The Romans believed it was bad luck for someone to enter a house with their **left** foot first. To stop this they used to place a servant by the front door—hence the modern term "a footman"!

If you slam a door you could be in for a load of trouble because you might trap a spirit, if he was taken by surprise!

It is unlucky to meet or pass anyone on the stairs. But if you can't avoid it, you should pass the other person with your fingers crossed! Not very easy if you're carrying something but apparently this comes from the time when staircases were very narrow and if two people had to squeeze past each other they would lay themselves open to attack from behind!

It's unlucky to trip while going down stairs! (Which is pretty obvious if you fall and land on your nose!)

"Getting out of bed the wrong side" means getting out on the **left** because this side is associated with the devil! But if you can't avoid getting out on the left side (walls can get in the way sometimes) you can escape the bad luck by putting your **right** shoe and sock on first!

Some people in the North of England believe that you can avoid getting bed sores by putting two buckets of fresh spring water under the bed each day! This may sound like an awful lot of trouble, but don't try and cheat by using cold tap water, because that's worse than if you hadn't even bothered in the first place!

If you turn a mattress on a Friday or a Sunday you'll have a week of bad dreams!

Many people never get into bed without looking under it first! Apparently they are looking for the devil who seems to like hiding under beds—though who knows what they'd do if they saw something!

If you want to live a long life you should position your bed so your head is pointing **south**! If you want to be rich your head should be pointing **east**, and for travel pointing **west**!

If you drop your books on the way to school it means you're going to make some mistakes in your lessons! Luckily it's only Americans who still believe this one. On the other hand, it's quite a good excuse for bad work—or is it?

Always carry at least one penny with you to help your luck. Also, if you go on a boat you must toss one penny over the bows of the ship as you leave port. This will stop bad weather.

It's bad luck to sew anything onto something that you are actually wearing, or to sew something new onto anything old. But if you are sewing and your thread gets tangled, then whoever owns the garment you are mending, is in for a healthy and wealthy life!

If you knock over your chair when getting up after a meal, this is a sign that you were telling lies during the conversation! (And of great clumsiness!)

You'll also be in for some back luck if you trip over a paving stone and don't go back and step over it properly!

If you go out for a walk with a friend and have to part company to walk either side of an obstacle, this means the two of you'll have a quarrel, unless one of you perks up smartly with the words **"Bread and butter"**!

If you can get hold of a hollow glass walking stick and having filled it with coloured sand, hair or white beans, place it over your front door, any evil spirit that enters your house to cause mischief will be so fascinated by looking at it that he'll forget why he called!

If you drop a towel or dishcloth when you are washing up you'll soon have a visitor! If you don't fancy a visitor right that minute, you can break the spell by quickly stepping over the cloth backwards!

If you drop a spoon and it lands with the bowl **upwards** then you're in for a surprise. But if it lands with the bowl facing **down** then I'm afraid you're in for a disappointment!

19

MING
WHO?

If you drop a plate or cup when washing up then you can guarantee that two more pieces of crockery will be smashed before the end of the day! One way round this is to find an old chipped piece of crockery and smash it deliberately, before you drop something a bit more valuable! (Better check that the old piece isn't a priceless antique before you try this out or you might get into worse trouble!)

If you go round to a friend's house for a meal, what you must never do when you've finished is fold up your napkin or place your chair back against the wall! If you do you'll never be invited there again!

If you drop a pair of scissors, it's very bad luck to pick them up straightaway. Best thing is to get someone else to pick them up for you. But if you're alone, you should step on them gently before picking them up, then rub them in your hands until they are warm before you use them again!

Many people believe that if you wash every part of your body, you are washing your luck away. In Wales many miners believed this, so deliberately left their backs dirty because they were convinced that if they were completely clean the mine roof would fall in on them. (Sounds like a convenient superstition for hot water haters!)

Hungarians believe that you can become very beautiful if you have a bath in human blood!

There's a British superstition that if you look at someone through a piece of glass which is broken you will very soon quarrel with them!

TRA-LA-LA.
OH, WHAT A
BEAUTIFUL
MORNING, OH
WHAT.....

When you get up in the morning and have your first wash, if you splash the water all over the place you're going to have a good day! (Unless you get caught and have to spend the next half hour clearing up the mess!)

A very famous superstition is the one that you'll have seven years bad luck if you break a mirror! But what you may not know is that the English have a way of avoiding that bad luck! If you pick up all the bits of broken glass and throw them into a river all the bad luck will be washed away! (And the evidence!)

Many old people go to bed wearing garters made out of cork because cork is supposed to be a cure for cramp!

It is unlucky to have just three lights on in any room in your house!

When a bride is all dressed up for her wedding it is very bad luck for her to look at herself in a mirror. The only way to avoid the bad luck is if her outfit is not complete, for example if she takes one shoe off!

If you find a piece of cotton sticking to your clothes you are going to receive an important letter, and if you examine the cotton closely, you may be able to see (in the way it is lying) the shape of the initial of the letter writer!

Nowadays, **"laying a table"** means putting the knives and forks by the side of each place. This is because meal times are supposed to be friendly occasions. This superstition dates from olden days when a man never put his knife down while eating in case someone attacked him. Therefore, the only sign he could make that he was feeling safe and friendly was when he did put his knife down.

If you find a pin lying on the ground it is only good luck if the point is facing away from you!

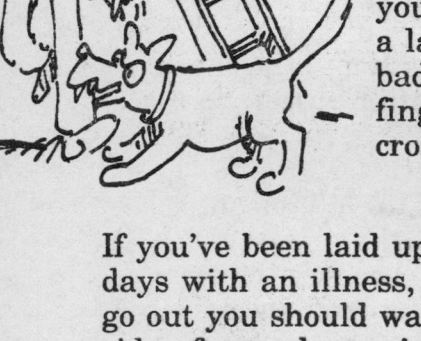

A very popular superstition is the one about not walking under ladders. This comes from the fact that in olden days when people were hung on gallows, a ladder was propped up against the top beam for the unfortunate victim to climb up to reach the rope!

If you're walking along the street and there is no way you can avoid walking under a ladder, you can beat the bad luck by crossing your fingers and keeping them crossed until you see a dog!

If you've been laid up in bed for a few days with an illness, the first day you go out you should walk round the outside of your house in the direction of the sun to make sure you get completely better!

If the initials of your name spell a word, the Americans believe you will be rich! (What about **Paul O**swald **O**liver **Rob**erts?)

If you have a bad dream you can wipe out any chance that it might come true by spitting three times as soon as you wake up! (A certain well-known dog must be a very poor sleeper!)

Many Scottish fishermen nail a horse-shoe to the mast of their boats to keep away storms!

A lucky horseshoe must be hung on your wall with the points **facing up**, because if they face down the good luck will **"run out"**!

If you find a horseshoe you should pick it up, spit on it then throw it over your **left** shoulder as you make a wish! As long as you don't hit someone, your wish will be granted!

If a pile of soot falls down your chimney someone in the house is coming into some money! (You'll probably have to spend it cleaning up the mess!)

To make sure that a baby will rise in life when it has grown up, the first time it is taken out of the room in which it was born, it must be taken up a flight of stairs! If it was born in a room on the top floor, the nurse should stand on a chair and lift the baby as high as possible! (Without dropping it, preferably!)

You mustn't cut a baby's nails before it is one year old or it will grow up **"light-fingered"**! (That means a thief not an electrician!)

In some parts of the country, mothers tie a bit of a rowan tree round their baby's neck so that the fairies won't have the power to swop it with one of their own!

If a baby laughs with its hands **open** it will grow up to be a generous person. But if it's fists are tightly **clenched** it will grow up mean!

26

TO EAT OR NOT TO EAT, THAT IS THE QUESTION!

If you drop a piece of bread and butter and it lands buttered side up, it means you're going to have a visitor! (If it lands the other way up you just get a messy table!)

If you should happen to want to find a dead body in a river, all you do, according to the American Indians, is weight a loaf with quicksilver and drop it into the river! It will float along and stop over the place where the dead body is! Believe it or not, this has been tried in the British Isles with some success!

A European custom says that bread baked on Christmas Eve will never go mouldy!

You must never stir a drink with a knife or you'll get stomach-ache!

It's bad luck to collect eggs and bring them into the house after dark! (You might also trip on the way and smash the lot!)

Sailors don't mention eggs by name when they're at sea, they call them **"roundabouts"**!

When you've finished a boiled egg you must turn it upside down and smash the bottom with your spoon! Better still crush it all into tiny pieces! It might make a mess, but it'll stop the witches picking up the empty shells, and using them to sail out to sea, where they sink the boats of honest sailors!

H.M.S. OMELETTE

If you throw an empty egg shell onto the fire, the hen who layed it will never lay another egg again!

If you want to dream of your true-love, you must hard boil an egg, take out the yolk and put salt in its place, then eat it on your own for supper! (It's more likely you'll have a nightmare!)

The Japanese believe that if a woman steps over an egg shell, she'll probably go mad!

If you spill some salt you must immediately throw a pinch of it over your **left** shoulder! You must do this because evil spirits always lurk behind your left shoulder watching what you are doing. This way the salt will go in their eyes and they won't be able to see to take advantage of your accident!

12,000,621,
12,000,622,
12,000,623

SALT

You should give a new born baby some salt to keep away evil spirits! Apparently, before they can get up to any mischief they have to count every grain of salt and as this takes a very long time they never have the chance to do a dirty deed!

There are still people in Britain and Europe who carry a pinch of salt in their hand when out at night, to protect themselves from evil spirits who lurk in the darkness!

Some Europeans sprinkle salt on the steps of a new house to keep evil spirits away!

If you use tea made from sage leaves as an eye-wash, your eyes will become wonderfully clear and bright!

A fresh sage leaf rubbed on ugly dark teeth will make them beautiful and white!

SAGE LOTION
SAGE CREAM

Bacon is a good cure for constipation! But only if it's been stolen!

Always remember to make a wish when eating new potatoes for the first time!

A good cure for rheumatism is to carry a potato in your pocket! But only one that has turned black and gone as hard as wood! (Rather uncomfortable when you sit down!)

Potatoes should never be planted on Good Friday because they just won't grow!

If you pick a pod with either nine peas in it or only one, this is good luck! You must then throw one of the peas over your right shoulder and make a wish!

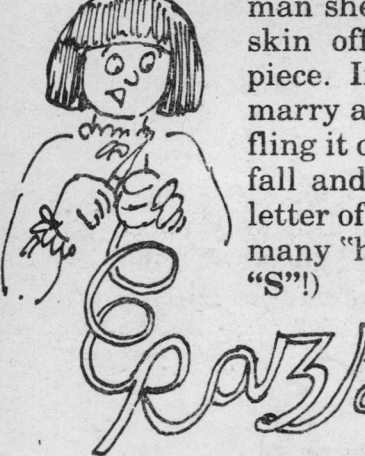

If a girl wants to find the name of the man she will marry, she must peel the skin off an apple in one continuous piece. If it breaks she isn't going to marry at all, but if it's whole, she must fling it over her left shoulder and it will fall and make the shape of the initial letter of her husband to be! (Funny how many "husband's to be" have the initial "S"!)

Carrots are supposed to be good for your eyesight! During the Second World War there was a great deal of publicity about British pilots being given a lot of carrots to eat to help them when flying at night. Actually the publicity was to hide the fact that the pilots were using Radar. But carrots do contain certain salts which have been proved to be good for your eyes!

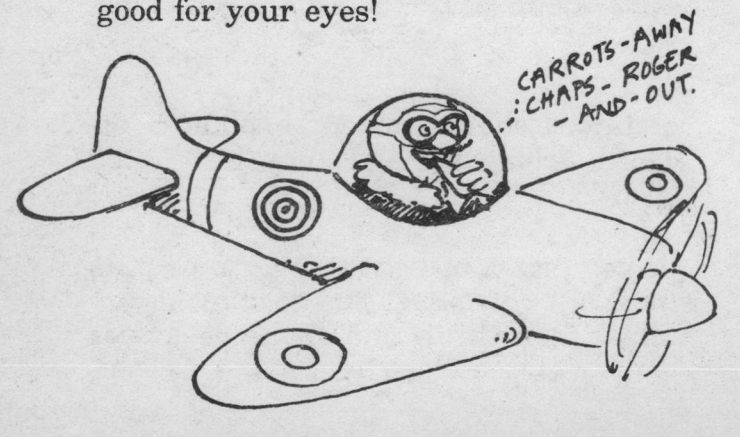

CARROTS - AWAY
CHAPS - ROGER
- AND - OUT.

Schoolboys who are about to be given a caning should rub an onion on their bottoms and they won't feel any pain! If they should have the luck to rub the onion on the actual cane, on the first stroke the cane will split in half!

Welsh soldiers always rub a leek all over their bodies before they go into battle to get extra strength and stop them from being wounded!

If a cheese is rubbed well with mint it will never go mouldy!

Eating fish will make you strong and wise!

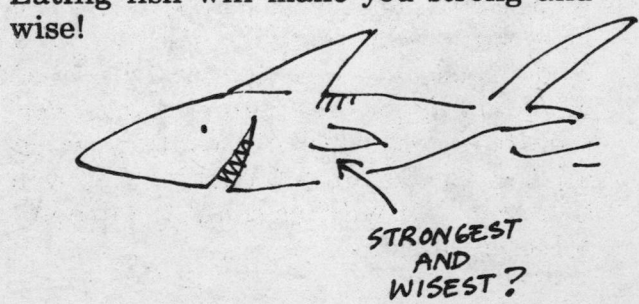

STRONGEST
AND
WISEST?

If you want to see your future you must eat a complete salted herring fish (bones and all) in three mouthfuls. Without taking a drink of water or speaking to anyone you must go immediately to bed—you will then dream of your future!

If you carry a root of chicory in your pocket you will become invisible!

But if that doesn't quite work, you can still carry a chicory root to help you open locks!

If you carry a nutmeg in your pocket you'll never get rheumatism or boils!

Nowadays we throw rice at a wedding (or confetti) but many years ago it was nuts! (How painful!)

In America if a young man is desperately in love, all he has to do to get the girl of his choice to fall in love with him is chew gum. He has to think about her and how much he wants her to love him then present her with the chewing gum. If she accepts it and chews it enthusiastically then he's won her!

A glutton is someone who eats far too much. In Canada they believe that if you can't make your finger and thumb meet around your wrist then you are a glutton!

The Welsh believe that drinking a spoonful of sea water every day will help you to live to a very old age! (Trouble is, it isn't clear whether they mean a teaspoon or a tablespoon!)

If the coffee pot rocks on the table, a visitor is coming! (Or the floorboards are loose!)

It's very bad luck to spill milk on the floor because fairies love milk and if they discover some spilt, they will take over your whole household!

If you make some tea much **weaker** than usual without meaning to do it, a friend is turning away from you! On the other hand, if you make it **stronger** without meaning to, you are going to make a new and very close friendship!

If the soup continues to boil after it has been taken off the heat, whoever is cooking it will live to a ripe old age!

If, when you open a tin of fruit, the juice splashes up into your face, something good is going to happen to you!

If a cork pops out of a bottle suddenly, you have a secret enemy!

If you drop any pudding which has eggs in it on the floor, someone is going to leave you a fortune!

Always pass the wine the "right" way round the table. It should follow the course of the sun!

If you eat goose at Michaelmas you won't be short of food for the whole of next year. This superstition comes from the fact that Queen Elizabeth I was eating a goose when she heard of Drake's victory over the Spaniards!

TO WEAR OR NOT TO WEAR, THAT IS ANOTHER QUESTION!

WHAT THE WELL-DRESSED PHANTOM FLAN FLINGER ABOUT TOWN IS WEARING THIS YEAR.

When you buy, or are given, something new to wear, you must always put a coin in the right hand pocket. If you don't, every time you wear it you won't have any money!

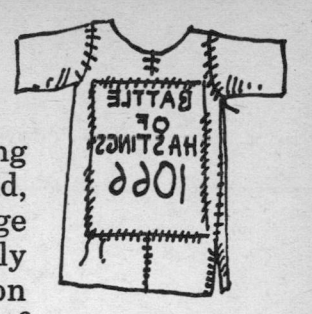

It's very lucky to put a piece of clothing on inside out! You may look a bit odd, but to keep the luck you mustn't change it until the time you would normally have taken it off. This superstition started when William put his shirt of mail on back to front just before the Battle of Hastings. His servants thought this was a sign of bad luck, but he, quickly, said it was a good luck omen and he wasn't going to change it till after the Battle. It worked!

In America girls believe that to have a happy Spring they must wear **THREE** new things on Easter Day!

It's unlucky to do your buttons up the wrong way! You must undo them all and start again!

Also, you mustn't put your **left** arm or leg or foot into anything first! You must always start with your right side!

Putting a hat or cap on back to front means bad luck! (Specially if it's a balaclava!) The only remedy is to buy a new one!

In Russia, if someone robs your house
and leaves some part of their clothes
behind, you must beat it with a stick!
The burglar will then fall ill and the
police will be able to catch him easily!

Wearing a diamond ring will keep
witches away from you and also stop
you from going mad!

Shoes can cause a lot of problems! It's
bad luck to:—Put them on a table; leave
them crossed or upside down on the
floor; put them on the wrong feet; or try
and walk with only one shoe on! (You
might also fall flat on your face!)

Many northerners believe that the first
time you put on something new you
should get a friend to pinch you!

If you burn an old shoe in your house it will get rid of all germs! (And the family!)

If you want to become invisible all you've got to do is wear a piece of jewellery that has an opal in it! Or so a thirteenth century chemist called Albertus Magnus believed!

If you want to remember something very important, there's an old saying that you should tie a knot in a handkerchief. This derives from the belief that a knot keeps away evil spirits. Apparently, the evil spirit becomes so fascinated by the sight of you tying the knot, that he'll forget that he was going to bother you!

If you leave your gloves behind at a friends' house you have to follow an extremely odd pattern of behaviour when you go back to collect them or you will offend the Gods of good fortune! When you re-enter their house you must immediately sit down. You can then pick up the gloves but you mustn't put them on until you are standing up and ready to leave!

If you make your mind up to do something, but are still a bit worried that it might not be the right decision, there's a very easy way to find out what you should do by counting your buttons! There's an old Jewish custom that if you have an even number of buttons then you've made the right decision, but if there's an odd number then you've made a bad mistake!

If your jewellery is a bit dirty, then the way to make them shine again is to put them in honey!

Apart from looking very odd, it's very unlucky to wear one brown shoelace and one black one!

If you buy yourself a nice new pair of sandals, you must put them on for the first time either in the morning or early afternoon! For some reason or other the Japanese believe that if you leave it till after five o'clock then you won't have much fun when you're wearing them!

If you wear your shoes out on the **inside** before the **outside** it shows you are a mean and stingy person! If you wear out the **outside** first you are extravagant!

If your shoelaces come undone it means that someone is talking about you! If it's the **right** one then you can smile because nice things are being said, but if it's the **left** lace you'll know that someone's being rather nasty about you!

43

EYE EYE!

THE NEWS WILL BE READ BY THE
<u>SPEC</u>TACULAR TREVOR MACDOUGHNUT

Did you know that tradition says you can tell a person's character by the colour of their eyes? You didn't! Read on and find out if you're a nice (or nasty) person.

Dark blue = delicate and refined
Light blue to grey = strong and healthy
Green = hardy
Hazel = vigorous and deep-thinking
Black = deceitful
Grey = greedy

If your **right** eye tickles then you're about to be lucky. If your **left** eye tickles—stand by for a rotten time!

But if your left eye continues to tickle, you can cure it by bathing the eye in rainwater collected from the leaves of a teazel plant!

Some English country folk believe you can cure a stye in the eye by rubbing it gently with a small piece of gold! (If you're fortunate to have an ingot or two lying around!)

Eye-brows that meet in the middle are supposed to be a sign of a jealous person—they also might be a werewolf! Or just a rotten liar!

IS THERE ANYONE THERE?

People with different coloured eyes, or ones set very close together, are supposed to have the Evil Eye. If you think they have some evil intent against you, one cure is to spit in their eyes three times! (Then they certainly will!)

HE NOSE YOU KNOW!

You can also tell a person's character by their nose.

Prominent = intelligence and determination
Thin = jealous and uncertain
Receding = bad tempered and obstinate
Tip-tilted = bright and lively

HE NOSE YOU KNOW!

"You'll be mad,
See a stranger,
Kiss a fool,
Or be in danger."

A tickling nose in America means you can expect a kiss; in Europe—a fight; in Britain—a letter; in Canada you're given a choice.

If a girl has a nose bleed in front of a boy (or the other way round) it means they are in love!

One drop of blood from the left nostril is a sign of good luck, but a flood means a bad day! (It's also very messy!)

47

Two "delightful" cures
for nose bleeds!

You must spear a toad with a knife and
then wear the corpse in a little bag
around your neck!

Poke a cat's tail up your nostril!

But if that doesn't work (or the cat isn't
happy) place a small wad of newspaper
beneath your upper lip!

YAAAAAAAAAAA

A MOUTH FULL OF TROUBLE!

OOOOOOOKAAA

You can also get a slight guide to someone's character by studying their teeth!
A large gap between the front two = lucky
Large = physical strength
Small and regular = careful and methodical
Teeth set wide apart in your jaw = you'll have to live away from your birth-place to make a successful career.

Some Americans believe it's bad luck to dream their teeth are falling out!

To cure toothache you must take a few strands of your hair and some nail clippings and nail them to an oak tree! This will "drive away" the pain.

49

You'll never guess what's in my bag!

To stop yourself getting toothache you should wear a little bag around your neck containing either a tooth from a corpse, or the forelegs and one hind leg from a mole!

If your lips tingle you're going to get kissed!

If you bite your tongue while you are eating you have recently told a lie!

A pimple on the tongue also means you've been telling lies!

It's unlucky to sing in bed, at the table, or in the street! (And anywhere else if you're tone deaf!)

If two people say exactly the same thing at the same time they must make a silent wish then link little fingers and say out loud the name of a poet! You may feel rather silly doing it but the wish should come true?

If your foot goes to sleep you can wake it up by spitting on a finger!

50

Germans believe that if you swear you increase the number of mice in your district!

If you forget what you're saying half way through a story it's a good sign that you're telling a lie!

When you yawn you should always cover your mouth with your hand to stop evil spirits leaping into your body! (It's also polite.) The North American Indians also say you should snap your middle finger and thumb at the same time! (Presumably not with the hand that's covering your mouth or you'd hit yourself on the face!)

If you sneeze while you're talking it shows you're telling the truth!

If you sneeze before breakfast you're going to get a present!

EAR EAR!

Did you know you can tell a person's character by looking at their ears? Here's what to look for.

Small = mean
Large = generous
Thin and angular = bad tempered
Long or prominent = musical
Large ear lobes = clever (the larger the smarter!)

If your **right** ear tingles, someone is saying nice things about you. If your **left** ear tingles they are saying nasty things about you.

Earrings worn in pierced ear lobes will cure bad eyesight!

The Dutch believe that if your left ear tingles, all you've got to do is bite your finger and the person who is saying nasty things about you will instantly bite their tongue!

Wearing earrings stops the devil entering your body through your ears!

Many sailors believe that wearing gold earrings will save them from drowning! (Small ones of course!)

LET'S GET A HEAD!

Now study your brow or forehead.
A high and wide brow = intelligent
A full brow over the temple = artistic
and imaginative
Rounded brows = able to reason and
work things out
Bulging forehead = slow thinking but
gets there in the end
Smooth forehead = good tempered
Deep lines in the forehead = real
thinker
A lot of short lines in forehead
quick tempered
**Deep lines in the forehead pointing
down to the root of the nose** = =
concentration which leads to success
**One line coming down between the
eyebrows** = dignified

Now your chin.

A large, well-shaped chin which is hollow in the center = generous and a love of fair play

A very pointed chin = crafty

A round, plump chin = cheerful, talkative and easy to live with

A long flat chin = good natured but lazy

Your head must measure at least 32 cms all the way round if you are going to be a successful person!

If you have a mole in the middle of your forehead you will be very rich! If you have one just above the temple you are full of wit and understanding!

HAIR TODAY GONE TOMORROW!

You've all probably heard of the superstition that men with hairy chests are supposed to be strong, and that people with red hair have quick tempers? Well here are some **hairy** tales that will really make your hair curl!

It's unlucky to **comb** your hair at night—although you can use a brush!

If you throw away some loose hair and a bird picks it up to use in its nest—you're going to get a headache!

It's unlucky to cut your **own** hair—not for *you* but for anyone you meet!

The Indians claim that a man without any hair on his chest either is, or will be, a thief!

Some Americans think that thinning hair is caused by a hatband that's too tight!

Also in America it's widely believed that baldness can be cured by shaving the head very closely!

I AM NOT ACTUALLY BALD... ...JUST MAKING SURE THAT I WON'T GO BALD!

If your hair starts turning grey, it's no use pulling the hairs out—every one you pull out will cause ten more to grow!

A comb made out of the wood from the rosemary plant will make your hair grow!

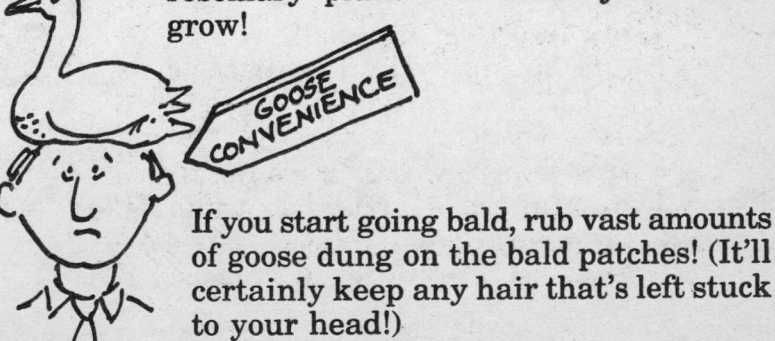

GOOSE CONVENIENCE

If you start going bald, rub vast amounts of goose dung on the bald patches! (It'll certainly keep any hair that's left stuck to your head!)

I'VE GOT TO HAND IT TO YOU!

Another way to tell what you are like, is to look at your hands, fingers and nails.

Thick hands = a strong character
Small, slender hands = weak and timid
Long hands = innocent
Short hands = careless and foolish
Hard hands = rude
Soft = witty
Hairy = person who likes luxury
Long fingers = artistic, but unable to save money
Short and thick fingers = moody and silly

Crooked little finger = wealthy
If forefinger is longer than the second = dishonest
More than five fingers = very lucky
(Except when buying gloves!)
Crooked nails = greedy

A tickle on your **left** hand means trouble, but you can break this spell by rubbing your hand quickly on a piece of wood!

If two friends wash their hands in the same basin of water they will soon quarrel—unless you spit in the basin!

If you pull your finger joints and they make a cracking sound, then you know that somebody loves you!

It's unlucky to cut your nails on Friday or Sunday, although Monday and Tuesday are all right!

If a would-be burglar wanted to commit a crime without being detected, all he had to do was carry the hand of an executed criminal which was cut from his body while still on the gallows! (Aren't many of those around nowadays!)

White spots on your finger nails also have different meanings;

Little finger = a journey
Ring finger = money
Middle finger = a new enemy
First finger = a new friend
Thumb = a present

Americans believe that if you put your thumb into your mouth and press it against the roof it will cure your headache!

It's unlucky to meet a left-handed person on a Tuesday!

When saying goodbye to a group of people, if you should shake someone's hand twice you should do it a third time to ward off back luck!

If you place your hands into water that has been used for boiling eggs you will get warts!

But you can get rid of warts by putting some pebbles and a coin in a small bag and leave it in the middle of the road. If someone picks it up and keeps the coin they'll keep the warts as well!

If you tickle a baby it will grow up with a stutter!

CREATURE FEATURE!

A child can be cured of whooping cough if it's put on the back of a donkey and walked round in a circle nine times!

The donkey got its name because it behaved very stupidly in the Garden of Eden. When Adam had given all the creatures their names, God asked them what they were? When the donkey couldn't remember his, Adam pulled and pulled at his ears saying **"Donkey! Your name is Donkey!"** Which also explains why the donkey has such long ears!

When a donkey brays and twitches its ears, bad weather is on the way!

When a pig runs about its sty with straw in its mouth there is a storm on the way!

In Britain's it's believed that if a wolf sees a man before the man sees it, the unlucky man will be struck dumb!

If you say the word **"wolf"** during December you are likely to get attacked by one!

If you are going to visit someone who isn't very well, if you pick up a stone and there is a worm underneath, they will get better! If there is no living thing underneath then that person isn't going to improve!

The cat is the most famous animal so far as superstitions are concerned. This dates back to the Romans and Persians who held them in great awe, and the Egyptians who regarded the cat as a God—Bast, the Cat-Goddess. Because of this Pagan belief, during the sixteenth and seventeenth century when all the witch hunts took place, it was believed that witches could turn themselves into cats.

In Britain a **black** cat is supposed to be **lucky**, but most other countries regard them as **unlucky**. In both America and Europe a **white** cat is also unlucky!

If a cat sneezes it either means that good luck for the household is on the way—or it means rain! But if it sneezes three times then someone in the family will get a cold. (What about "cofing" cats?)

A cat sitting with its back to the fire means a storm is on the way, while a cat sharpening its claws on a table leg means the weather's going to get better.

It's unlucky to hear a cat crying as you are about to set off on a journey—you must return and find out what's the matter. (It probably wants to be let out!)

A cat that has been **bought** will be absolutely useless at catching mice.

If a **black** cat crosses your path you will do well in whatever you are doing at that moment, but if it's a **white** one you'd better go straight home because your business will fail!

If a black cat enters your house, luck will come in with it. You shouldn't drive it away but feed it and make it welcome!

If a black cat enters a theatre during a rehearsal, the play will be a success!

If you meet a frog in the middle of a road you will shortly get some money!

If you eat a hare you will become a happy cheerful person who is nice to know! (Except among hares!)

If a man wears a waistcoat made from the skin of a hare, he will walk erect and straight however long he lives!

If a hare is seen outside a building in the day time, a fire will break out in that place before night-time!

The Scots believe that cows should be tarred behind the ears and at the root of the tail or the witches will steal their milk.

Cows feeding on high ground means good weather's on the way, but if they hold their tails upright or slap them against a fence, or feed huddled together, rain is on the way.

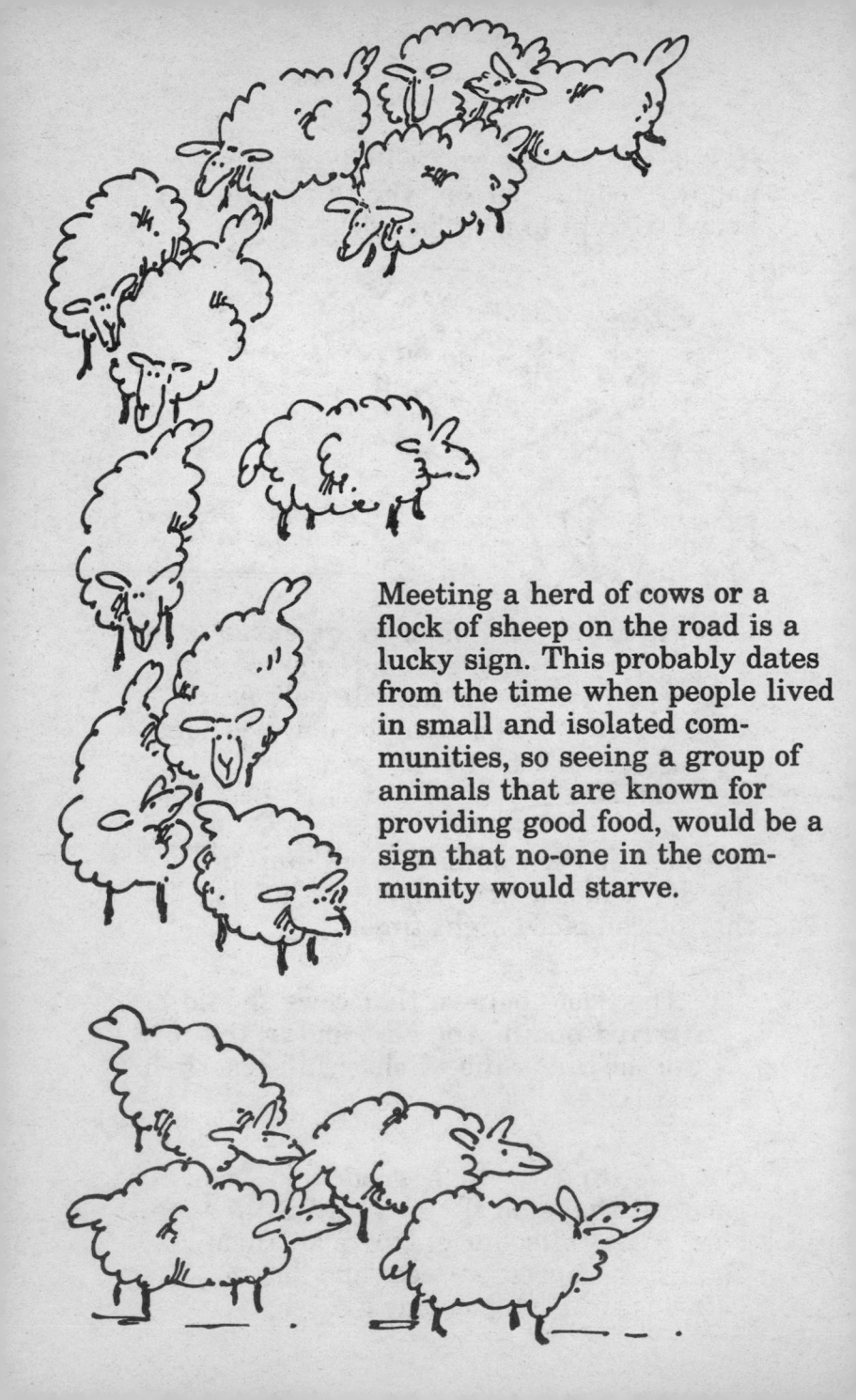

Meeting a herd of cows or a flock of sheep on the road is a lucky sign. This probably dates from the time when people lived in small and isolated communities, so seeing a group of animals that are known for providing good food, would be a sign that no-one in the community would starve.

On Christmas day sheep are supposed to bow three times to the East. This is because they are remembering the cattle who were in the stable at Bethlehem and watched whilst Jesus was being born!

In Europe a **black** sheep is supposed to bring good luck to the flock, which is rather opposite to the phrase **"black sheep of the family"** which usually means someone who is bad!

Some shepherds still believe that when they die they must have a tuft of wool in their coffins. This way, when they get to heaven they won't have to go before God to tell him what they've been up to, because no shepherd would leave his flock!

If you want to gamble or make a bet, make sure you have a tooth of a badger in your pocket then you won't lose!

The horse has always been regarded as an important animal which probably dates from Greek times when the animal was worshipped as the God Artemis. Mainly they are regarded as lucky, but sometimes they are a bad omen.

Some English country folk are said to be scared of *white* horses and if they meet one on a journey they will spit on the ground to ward off the bad luck!

A horse with a white stocking is lucky, and if it has also got a white star on its forehead then its doubly lucky!

The people who live in the Ozark Mountains, central America, believe that if they hold up a piece of cloth of their chosen colour in front of a mare that's about to give birth, the colt will be that colour! (What if it's patterned?)

Nowadays a horse's mane is plaited to make it look smart, but it used to be done to keep away witches!

Americans think one of the worst signs of bad luck is if a red-haired girl on a white horse passes in front of them!

THE DEVIL'S BARBER SHOP.

The goat carries a lot of superstition because of its association with the Devil, and also the God Pan. Some people believe that because of this, you'll never see a goat constantly for twenty four hours because at some time it has to visit it's master—the Devil! The goat pays homage to the Devil who then combs its beard!

Despite this, the goat is also connected with good luck! Sailors believe that a goat skin hung from their mast will guarantee a calm voyage!

Some Europeans and Americans believe that if a goat is attracted into the grounds of a house where someone is ill and urged to eat as much grass as possible, if it is then driven out of the grounds it will take the sickness with it!

A goat's foot or some hairs from its beard are also used as lucky charms!

In France it's believed that if a lizard runs over a woman's hand, she will become very good at sewing!

If you swallow some baby frogs before breakfast you will be cured of consumption! (That means tuberculosis—but it could also put you off 'consuming' your breakfast!)

You probably know the expression **"crocodile tears"** which is a sign of someone being insincere or not meaning what they say! Well here's where it may have come from. The Indians believe the superstition that crocodiles make a sort of moaning sound to attract their victims. When they catch them they cheerfully eat the body, then they shed their famous "tears" over the victim's head before swallowing it to finish off their meal!

If you carry the right eye of a bat it will make you invisible!

One way to get rid of warts is to spear a frog and rub it on them! When the poor creature dies the warts will disappear!

There's an ancient belief that witches can disguise themselves as hares so it's very bad luck to see one **crossing** your path! On the other hand it's good luck to see a hare running **ahead** of you! This last superstition came true when Queen Bodicea went into a battle against the Romans. At first things were going badly for her but as soon as she saw a hare running ahead of her the battle switched in her favour and she came out victorious!

If you've got an ulcer the best way to cure it is to eat the tongue of a dog!

If you see a dog eating grass, rolling on the ground or scratching itself, then bad weather is on the way! (On the other hand it might just have an itch!)

When the squirrel was first created it had a very small and thin tail, but when it was in the Garden of Eden it was so horrified by the sight of Adam and Eve eating the famous apple that it tried to pull his tail across it's eyes to hide the sight. As a reward, God made his tail the long and bushy one that we know today. For this reason there is a superstition that if anyone shoots a squirrel they will have a lot of bad luck and will also find that they can no longer shoot straight!

Sailors believe that if they see rats leaving their ship, they also ought to leave pretty fast as it's a sign that their ship is going to sink!

Rats are famous for having very strong teeth. If *you* want good strong teeth then the next time one falls out (instead of putting it under your pillow for the fairies) throw it away with a request to the rats to **"send a stronger one"** in its place!

If a mouse nibbles someone's clothes during the night that person will suffer a misfortune! (Yes, they'll have holes in their clothes!)

If you have measles or whooping cough you'll be pleased to hear about an old folk cure which tells you to eat fried, roast or baked mouse!

If you see a mouse as you are about to set out on a journey you'd do better to go back indoors because it won't be a very successful journey if you carry on regardless!

Mice are supposed to be the souls of people who have been murdered, so if you want to rid your house of them all you have to do is hold one by its tail in front of a fire and as it starts to roast all the rest will run away! (Not surprising!)

On the first day of the month you should say **"white rabbits"** three times as soon as you wake up! If you do you'll have a jolly good month!

If a gardener uses a rabbit's foot to carry pollen from one fruit tree to another his trees will flourish!

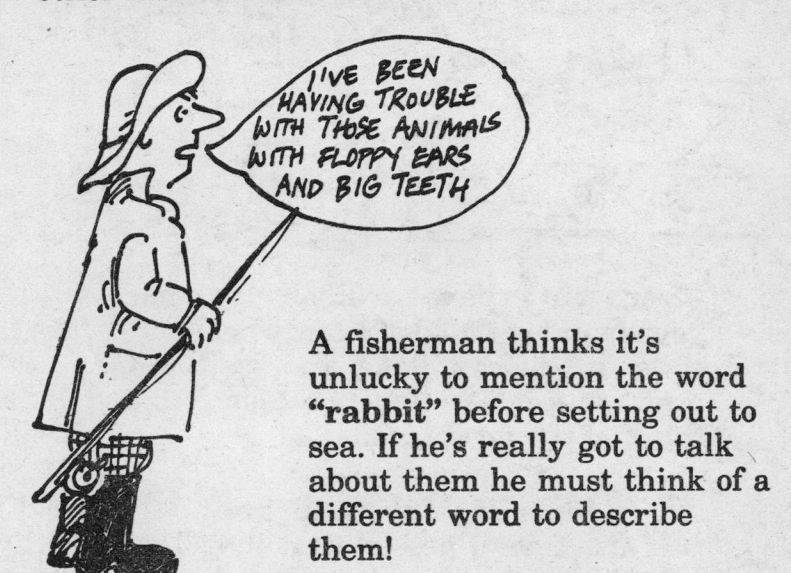

I'VE BEEN HAVING TROUBLE WITH THOSE ANIMALS WITH FLOPPY EARS AND BIG TEETH

A fisherman thinks it's unlucky to mention the word **"rabbit"** before setting out to sea. If he's really got to talk about them he must think of a different word to describe them!

Many poachers carry a rabbit's foot in their pockets because they believe it'll stop them from getting caught!

If you make cattle step over an axe the first time they go out to pasture they will never be bothered by witches!

It's very bad luck for a duck to lay a dun coloured egg, unless you kill the duck immediately and hang it upside down! (It's still bad luck for the duck!)

If you want to have a really happy home you should get hold of a few wheel-barrows full of cow dung and scatter it round your house! (Ignore the smell and think of the good luck!)

In India they believe that cow dung can also cure illnesses! (But they don't say exactly what you've got to do with it!)

A black snail should be picked up by its horns as soon as you see it and thrown over your left shoulder. Good luck will follow immediately!

You can cure a cough by boiling three snails in barley water then give the drink to the sufferer! Apparently this cure will only work if the sufferer doesn't know what he or she is drinking! (Hardly surprising. If they knew they wouldn't touch the stuff!)

CREEPY CRAWLY
CORNER

If you'd like to have a fabulous singing voice, all you've got to do is copy an old American Indian recipe! Catch three crickets, crush them, boil them in water then drink the revolting result!

Yorkshire people believe that if you find a hairy caterpillar, to bring good luck you should fling it over your left shoulder!

If a fly falls into the glass you're drinking out of you'll have good luck! (As long as you don't swallow the fly!)

If you carefully air your bed on the Thursday before Easter you'll never get any fleas in it!

If you find an ant's nest by your back door, (although you may trip over it or find them crawling under your kitchen door) it is in fact a good sign and a lot of money is coming your way!

MONEY COMING

In the Middle Ages the houses which were full of spiders were where the healthiest people lived! That may sound odd (and not much fun if you don't like spiders) but flies carry a vast amount of disease, and spiders are the most efficient way of getting rid of them—by catching them in their webs!

I WISH SHE WOULD GET ON WITH THAT WEB —I'M SO COLD

If you see a spider actually spinning its web you will soon get some new clothes!

81

If a spider drops on your face or clothes you'll soon receive some money! Particularly if it's the red money spider.

If you cut yourself you can stop the bleeding by laying a cobweb over the wound! This is supposed to date back to the time when the baby Jesus was hidden by a web when Herod's soldiers were searching for him.

If you kill a spider it will very soon start to rain!

If someone is ill you must leave their curtains and windows open at night so that all the gnats can fly in! Apparently they will fly around collecting the illness then fly away taking the illness with them!

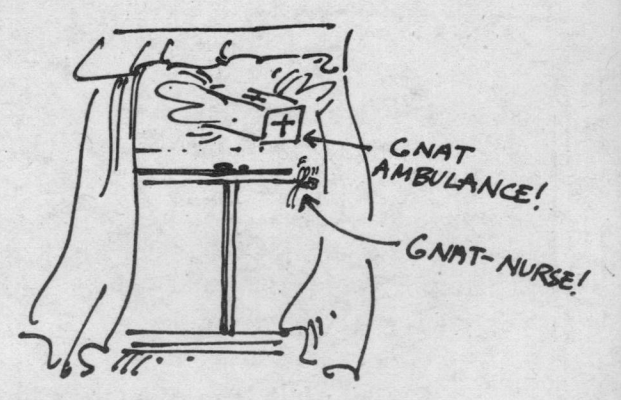

A bee sting will cure you of rheumatism!

So you see bees all things considered as I have explained in some depth I'm afraid there is no alternative. A move seems to be in order, so if...

Buzzz doesn't he go on?

If you want to move a hive of bees you must tell them what you are doing or they'll sting you!

Never move a hive of bees on a Good Friday or they will all die!

If a girl is going to be married she must go to her bee hive and whisper quietly **"Little Brownies, little Brownies, your mistress is to be wed."** (Bet she feels a fool!) But to make sure of the bees blessing she must give them a piece of her wedding cake!

Yum, yum we must keep this superstition going chaps.

The number of spots on a ladybird's back will tell you how many happy months are ahead of you!

It's very lucky for a ladybird to land on you—as long as you don't brush it off!

You must always be gentle with ladybirds because they are symbolic of the Virgin Mary! If one lands on you you should put it on the palm of your hand and say to it **"Ladybird, ladybird fly away home, your house is on fire and your children are gone."** It may not be a very nice thing to say to a ladybird, but because it will usually fly away as soon as you say this rhyme, it's supposed to show that Ladybirds can understand what we say! Actually, the reason it flies away is because it doesn't like standing on a hot, sweaty hand!

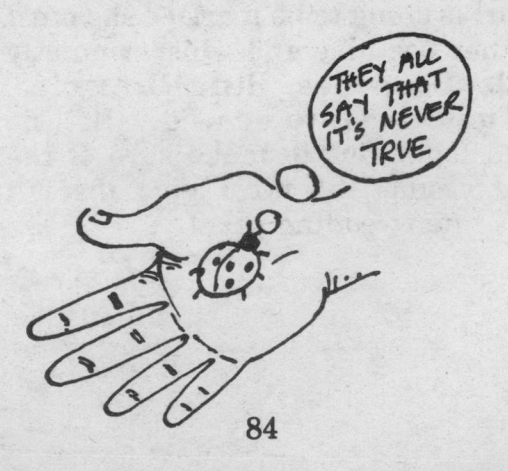

THEY ALL SAY THAT IT'S NEVER TRUE

A FLIGHT OF FANCY!

If you want to remain a happy and cheerful person, you mustn't look into an owl's nest because it'll make you miserable and unhappy for the rest of your life!

To see a magpie is considered very unlucky so many people in Britain take their hats off and give a little bow when the bird passes! Apparently this superstition comes from the time when Noah built his ark. All the animals and birds went into the ark except the magpie—it chose to perch on the roof outside!

Not a very happy superstition this, but if the very famous ravens who live at the Tower of London should fly away, the royal family will die and Britain will collapse!

If you see a group of pigeons sitting on your roof you'd better buy a new umbrella because it's about to start raining!

Staying with Noah and his ark, the first bird to be released when the ark reached dry land was the kingfisher! When it flew up into the sky it's old dull grey colour was transformed into a brilliant sky blue colour on the back, and the red of the sun on its breast! It's, therefore, a very lucky bird!

Good news for sailors!
When the kingfisher is sitting on its eggs there are no storms at sea! Also, if you should find some feathers or plumage from a kingfisher you should sew them into your clothes for good luck!

The first call the cuckoo makes in spring is always very exciting to hear!

But apparently the calls the cuckoo makes are all different, and all have different meanings for the people who are listening. People ask so many questions of the cuckoo that it spends all its time answering, which is why it hasn't time to build its own nests so lays its eggs in other birds' nests! (That's the cuckoos' excuse—other birds might feel differently!)

When you hear the first cuckoo in spring you should straightaway make a wish because it will very likely come true! But make sure you don't hear the first cuckoo when you're in bed, because if you do the next twelve months won't be much fun!

If the first cuckoo you see is standing still, so will you! But if it's flying it means that you will soon be moving house!

When you hear the first call of the cuckoo you should kiss your hand and wave it in the direction of the sound saying **"Cuckoo, tell me true, when shall I be married?"** Then you count the number of times the cuckoo calls continuously and this is the number of years to your wedding day!

"A whistling woman and a crowing hen is neither good for God nor men" is one of Britain's oldest superstitions.

It's very unlucky if your hen lays you an **even** number of eggs! Get rid of one of them as soon as possible!

COCK-A-DOODLE
DOO..OOOO.

If a hen crows it means its got
"the devil in her" and should be
killed before it starts breaking her
own eggs and teaching the other
hens to do the same!

If you see a group of hens huddled together on a bit of raised ground preen-
ing their feathers, or hear a cock crowing in the evening, bad weather is on
the way!

If one of your family isn't feeling too
well you can cure them by rubbing a
cockerel on their body. To make sure
that the disease, (or whatever) is defi-
nitely removed, you must throw the
cockerel into the sea or send it a long
way from the district!

In Ancient Greece the peacock was
kept in the temples of worship
and if someone stole one, (or even
just one of its feathers) they were
punished by death! This may
explain why nowadays it's
believed to be very unlucky to have
peacock feathers in the house, and
disastrous as a dress decoration!

If bird droppings land on you it's a sign of bad luck! (There's a surprise!)

It's unlucky if a bird flies into your house through an open window!

When a cock crows with its head facing the door of your house you'd better start dusting because a visitor is on the way!

When you hear a crow cawing you must measure the length of your shadow with your footsteps by placing one foot in front of the other! Count the steps, add thirteen, then divide the whole by six. If you're left with one you will have good fortune; two means sorrow; three means happiness; four means plenty of food, and five plenty of money!

It's very unlucky to see a crow standing on one leg, or two crows fighting near your house!

COMPOST CORNER!

If someone can't sleep, give them a bunch of primroses! (Though I'm not quite sure what you're supposed to do with them—knock them over the head perhaps?)

If you stare into the centre of a poppy you may go blind!

If you have a lousy memory wear a sprig of rosemary in your buttonhole and it'll help you to remember anything you want to!

If you hold a buttercup under your chin and a yellow glow shows on your skin it means you like butter!

If mint grows on your land in great quantities you are going to be wealthy!

If you get stung by a wasp or a bee you should rub the head of a marigold on the sting and the pain will vanish!

The Welsh say it is very lucky to find the first daffodil in Spring as this will bring you a lot of gold in the year to come!

If you catch a falling leaf in Autumn you won't get a cold all winter!

You can cure chilblains by pricking them with the spikes of a holly leaf! (Sounds more painful than suffering the chilblains!)

If you see the sun shining through the branches of an apple tree on Christmas Day you're going to get a bumper crop of apples! To make doubly sure you should put a piece of toast in the fork of the main branch!

If you put some hazel twigs in your hair and make a wish it will come true!

If you put a sprig of mistletoe at the foot of your bed you won't have any nightmares!

HERE IS THE WEATHER FORECAST!

If you've ever seen a person carrying the branches of a bay tree over their head during a storm, it's because they believe the bay tree will never be struck by lightning!

If you open all the doors and windows in your house during a storm it won't get hit by a thunderbolt—but you'll probably get exceedingly wet!

In parts of Austria and Germany it's still believed that you can stop a storm by opening a window, chucking out some grain and yelling **"There, that's for you—now cease!"**

You must never cut your hair or nails at any other time but during the night. You must then burn the clippings to stop the witches stealing them to stir up a storm!

The wives of sailors should never comb their hair when their husbands are at sea because the action will start a fearful gale!

If you see a new moon and the tips are pointing **up**, then the month ahead will be fine. But if the tips are pointing **down** then it's going to be dreadful weather!

If it rains on St Swithin's Day, July 15th, it's going to keep on raining for forty days! This superstition comes from the time when the body of St Swithin was buried by the door of Winchester Cathedral. Because it was a bit of a nuisance the monks decided to try and move it. But as soon as they started work on July 15th it started raining and continued for forty days. They decided St Swithin had sent the rain because he didn't want to be moved, so they gave up the idea—hence the superstition!

97

The best way to stop rain is to
say this rhyme;

**"Rain, rain go away,
Come again another day"**

or

**"Rain, rain go away,
Come again on washing
day"**

But rain water can also be
very lucky! If you wash
money in it it can never be
stolen (probably because the
note will disintegrate!) and
it's also a good cure for
sore eyes!

If there hasn't been any rain
for a long time you can make
it rain by burning ferns or
heather!

You will never be struck by
lightning when you are
asleep!

**"Red sky at night, shepherd's delight,
Red sky in the morning, shepherd's warning."**

We all know this rhyme, but unlike many other silly superstitions, this one actually works. If the sky is red at night then the next day is going to be fine. If the sky is red in the morning then it's going to be a pretty miserable day!

If you are frightened of being struck by lightning you can protect yourself by winding a snake skin round your head! (Remember to remove the snake first!)

If you find a garden rake which has fallen on the ground with its prongs pointing up, cancel any plans for going out the next day because it's going to bucket down with rain!

If you find a pine cone which is tightly closed up it's going to rain, but if it's wide open the weather will be fine!

To stop a rain storm you should send a first born child out into the garden with instructions to strip naked then stand on its head! (Might not work but it's good for a laugh!)

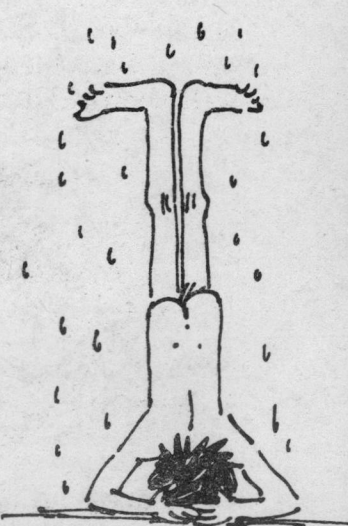

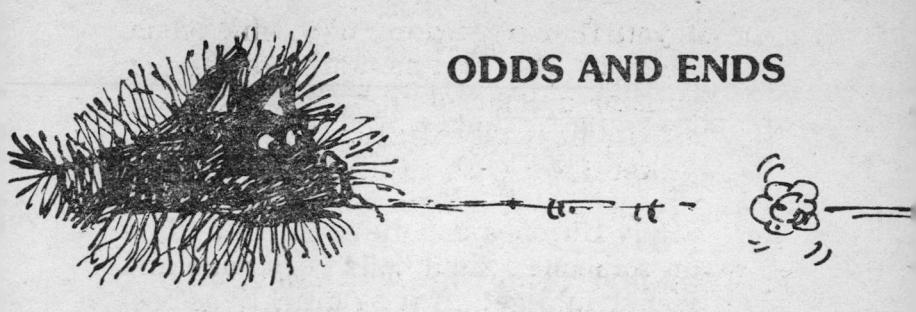

ODDS AND ENDS

If you see some bubbles floating on the top of your cup of tea or coffee your about to receive some money!

If you own a boat and you find barnacles on its bottom, watch out because they will soon turn into geese!

You must never talk when you are going under a railway bridge! Witches hide in the arches and will leap out at you if you're talking! This applies whether you're on foot or in a train!

Thieves will never steal a pack of cards because they believe that cards have the power to give them away!

Many Europeans believe that standing on someone's shadow is very rude and you should get off it as quickly as possible!

If someone waves a spade at you to attract your attention you are going to suffer some bad luck unless you immediately throw some earth at the person waving the spade!

Steeplejacks believe they will be safe from accidents if they tie a knot in their braces!

If you bang your elbow you must immediately bang the other one or you'll have bad luck!

If you've gone off someone and want to harm them, all you have to do is bite your own elbow and that person will be drenched in a thunder storm! (Have you ever tried biting your own elbow?)

If you find a lump of coal in the middle of the road you should throw it over your left shoulder then walk away without looking back!

The Welsh believe that rheumatism can be cured by making the sufferer strip naked then be buried up to the neck in a churchyard for two hours! This has to be done every day until the rheumatism goes! (Or the sufferer!)

You can also cure rheumatism by putting slices of green pepper under your nails; crawling through a gap in a bramble bush or making bees sting the affected parts of the body!

Carrying the knuckle bone of a leg of mutton will stop you getting sciatica!

If someone is ill you can cure them by passing their body through a natural hole in a tree or a rock!

You probably know the phrase **"Pinch me in case I'm dreaming."** Well many years ago when sailors used to be at sea for months at a time, when they got home their families might be so surprised to see them that they thought they were ghosts, so the sailors suggested **"pinch me"** to show they were real!

If you believe that thirteen is an unlucky number you suffer from **"triskaidekaphobia"**!

The woman who carries a baby to church to be christened should also carry a piece of bread and cheese to give to the first person she meets! If the gift is refused then the child will have an unhappy life!

Sand was once very popular for bringing good luck to a newly married couple! This comes from the old story about King Canute. One day after he came home from the sea-shore he sat down to shake the sand out of his shoes. A wedding party passed and the good king shook the sand out in front of the couple wishing them a happy marriage and as many children as there were grains of sand!

If you see the first star of the evening and instantly make a wish, as long as you keep the wish a secret and say out loud the following verse, the wish will come true!

**"Star light, star bright,
First star I see tonight,
I wish I may, I wish I might,
Have the wish I wish tonight."**

When you see a new moon you must put your hand in your pocket and turn over any coins that you have! If you do, by the time the next new moon appears that amount will have doubled!

If you're out in the open and see a new moon for the first time over your right shoulder you should quickly make a wish as it's bound to come true!

It's very rude to point at a star and as a punishment your finger will get stuck in that position!

If an American girl wants to meet her future husband she has to follow a very odd set of rules! She must stand by the side of the road and count ten red cars; she must then find a girl with red hair wearing a purple dress; after that she must find a man wearing a green tie; then, believe it or not, the very next man that she sees will be her future husband!

TODAY'S THE DAY!

CHRISTMAS

Everyone knows it's lucky to kiss under the mistletoe at Christmas, but did you know that the lucky man should pluck a white berry for every girl he kisses?

If you draw water from a clear well on Christmas Day you will be drawing good luck for everyone who drinks it!

If a girl wants to "see" her future husband, when she goes to bed on December 24th she should put her shoes across each other in the shape of a "T" and say;

"I hope tonight my true love to see—
So I put my shoes in the form of a
T!"

At Christmas you should always eat twelve mince pies to make sure you have twelve happy months! To really make this work you should eat one, but only one, each day from Christmas to Twelfth Night!

On Christmas Eve, if you leave a pile of salt on the table and next morning it's unchanged you'll have a great day! But if some of it has melted, Christmas Day won't be a lot of fun!

HALLOWEEN

If a girl wants to "see" her future husband on Halloween she must sit on her own before a mirror, and by the light of a candle eat an apple. Her sweetheart will appear behind her in the mirror. She must keep on eating the apple until it's finished. Then, and only then can she turn round—but she must blow the candle out first!

The next one needs a bit of courage! The girl opens a door, or gate, that leads into her garden and holding onto the end of a piece of cotton she must throw the cotton reel as far as she can into the darkness. A gentle pull will tell her that someone is on the other end! She then walks out into the garden winding the cotton round her wedding finger. She will eventually come face to face with her spectral lover! They must not speak to each other. The scary bit is that she mustn't tell anyone what she is doing either before or after the event!

Another way to see a future husband on Halloween is to carry a broken egg in a glass to a fresh-water spring. If you add some water to the glass and swirl the mixture around for a few moments, when the liquid settles you will see a picture of your "husband to be" as well as the children you are going to have!

TISWAS SPORTING TIPS!

PHANTOM FLAN FLINGERS
LINING UP FOR THE
'FLAN AND SPOON RACE!

You wouldn't believe how many superstitions surround sport, or how superstitious sportsmen and women are supposed to be!

It's unlucky for a river angler during
fishing to swop a rod or to change a
successful float for another which is
supposed to be the latest and the great-
est.

Spit is supposed to be so powerful that
you should spit on your bait before
throwing it out. If you don't, you won't
catch a single fish!

It's an ill omen to place the keep net in the water before catching your first fish!

It's bad luck to ask a fisherman how many fish he's caught because it will ruin his chances of catching any more!

No angler who sits on an upturned bucket will catch a single fish!

If you see a dragonfly hovering over the water when you're fishing, it's trying to tell you something! If you're a nice kind person it's pointing out where the fish are, but if you're a rotten old nasty it's showing you empty water!

It's unlucky for a **right-handed** fisherman to cast with his **left** hand, and also the other way round!

Scottish anglers believe that if they aren't having any luck they should throw another fisherman into the river and then haul him out! The fish are supposed to be so impressed that they try and copy what has happened!

It's unlucky for a fisherman to stop and count how many fish he's caught because he certainly won't catch any more!

If you see an earwig on your way to go fishing you're in for a good catch!

It's unlucky to say the word **pig** before you cast your line!

There are also many silly superstitions for those who fish at sea:

It's unlucky for a fisherman on the way to his ship to meet a woman wearing a white apron or someone who's cross-eyed! He should go home and wait for the next tide!

Yorkshiremen believe they must pay King Neptune for taking his fish! As the nets are being played out they cut a slice in one of the cork floats and insert a coin in it! When the cork has been underwater for a time, if the coin disappears it means Neptune will allow the fish to enter the nets because he's accepted payment for them!

Football is full of superstition. All the supporters who wear scarves, woolly hats and swing rattles are being superstitious because they're hoping their actions will bring some magic into their team's playing! Also, many teams have mascots to bring them luck!

Many players don't like being watched by their wives or girlfriends. This dates back to the time when people believed in witchcraft and that a woman could put the "evil eye" on someone simply by watching them!

In the dressing room it is an old custom for the oldest player to bounce a ball to the youngest player. For the team to have **good** luck, the youngest must catch the ball on the bounce! If he drops it—trouble!

Many players always put their **left** boot on first—apparently the good luck is in the **right** boot and must be put on last!

Many centre forwards bounce the ball on the centre spot three times before the kick off. Also, some goalkeepers kick or touch both of their goalposts as the match starts!

It's unlucky for a boxer to wear a new pair of boots when fighting an important contest. He also isn't at all happy if he sees a hat lying on a bed or couch before a fight!

Many years ago a champion boxer, who was defending his title, decided that it was unlucky to enter the ring first. He insisted that his opponent, the challenger, went in first. When the champion won the fight, it became a rule that the challenger always ducks under the ropes first.

WELL, YOU'VE HEARD OF BOXING BEARS.

When you see a boxer spitting on the palms of his gloves, he isn't being dirty, he's just warding off the gods of bad luck!

Many darts players waggle their left foot about on the line before they make a throw. Apparently this is to remove any nasty spirit that might be lying there ready to put him off his aim!

It's very bad luck in tennis to hold three balls when you're serving! You'll also see many superstitious tennis players refusing to use a ball for a second serve after they've just used it and had a fault!

117

Many yachtsmen will never remove the mast from their boat when it's in dry dock for the winter, without putting a silver coin in its place.

Others feel it's much better to come second or third in a heat for a major race because it might be tempting the gods too much to expect to come first twice running!

It's unlucky to whistle on board a ship unless it is becalmed, then it's considered lucky because of the phrase "whistle up the wind!" But if whistling doesn't work to raise a wind, a yachtsman can get out of calm trouble by scratching his fingernail on the mainmast!

Golfers seem to be surrounded by silly superstitions! Here are just a few of the silliest!
It's bad luck to approach a tee from the front; clean a ball when your game is going well; change your mind about a club once you've taken it out of the bag; or unwrap a new ball in the middle of a round—you should have done that before getting to the first tee!

118

On the other hand, many golfers think it's lucky to use a ball bearing the number three, five or seven; carry an old but popular club in their bag although they no longer use it; and to place the golf ball on a tee so that they can read the maker's name!

Cricketers seem to be one of the most superstitious groups of sportsmen! If a batsmen puts his pads on the wrong legs, although he changes them, he might as well not go out onto the crease because he certainly won't score any runs!

If two batsmen in the same team wash their hands at the same time before a match, they might as well go home because they're both going to be out for a duck!

If a batsman has to take guard twice at the **same** end, he might as well lay down his bat as he'll be bowled soon after!

119

If a batsman stumbles on the way from the pavilion to the crease he is certainly not going to score a century! In fact he may not score at all!

If a bowler has to restart his run, his captain ought to banish him to the furthest part of the field because he certainly won't bowl anyone out!

In horse racing there are also hundreds of silly superstitions! It's said to be lucky for a punter to meet a cross-eyed woman on the way to a race meeting; to pick a jockey who is wearing their favourite colours; and if you're the sort of person to gambol by putting a pin in a piece of paper, it's luckiest to use a pin that's been used to make up a wedding dress!

If you're betting on a horse you should never wish it, or the jockey, good luck before the race begins!

Never bet on a horse that's changed its name as it'll come last; fall at a hurdle; or simply give up half way round!

If a jockey drops his whip before a race he might as well go home, because he certainly won't win!

If a jockey sees his boots standing upright on the floor, he knows he's going to be unseated in his race!

No jockey likes to be called a jockey before a race. Unless he's called by his proper name he believes he won't stand a chance!

But it's always good luck to kiss a horse after its won a race because that will encourage it to go on and win more races!

When you play a game with dice, here are three ways to get good luck: rub the dice on the head of someone who's got red hair; snap your fingers to drive away evil spirits at the same time as blowing on the dice; or make sure you keep throwing sixes!

If you like playing card games but find you're losing, all you have to do is get up and walk three times round the table you are playing on; or ask a friend to change places with you. Trouble is, your friend might think your seat is unlucky so won't move, the only thing you can then do is turn your chair round and sit astride it; take out a handkerchief and sit on it; not sit with your legs crossed; or make sure when you shuffle the cards that you blow on them hard!

If you let a card fall on the floor, particularly a black one, you aren't going to win a game! But if you think a particular card is lucky for you, try and touch it with your second finger before the game starts and you might be on a winning streak!

If you're playing with a partner, the best thing to do for good luck is to stick a pin in them—no, not in **them** but in their clothes! But if you want to do really well with your partner you must make sure that neither of you sings or whistles!

TISWAS SILLY SUPERSTITION GAME

Finally, here's a game for you to play with your friends to find out what fortune has in store for you.

What you need are three dice and a flat table with a circle drawn in the middle—not a very large circle, about 12 inches across! Throw the dice on the table then add the numbers on the dice that land in the circle. (If all three dice land outside the circle you might as well go straight back to bed because you're going to have a rotten day!)

Look up your number in this chart and find out what's going to happen to you during the day.

ONE—Not a lot, in fact a rather boring day!

TWO—Slight trouble with hardly any good news but there's nothing to worry about!

THREE—Good. Seize the chance that comes today.

FOUR—A disappointment—but it will turn out for the best.

FIVE—News of a death but it's news you've been expecting.

SIX—A marriage. This will come as a great surprise if not distress.

SEVEN—An omen of good luck. You're worried about something but this number tells you everything is going to be alright.

EIGHT—Disagreeable news in the post. But don't worry there's better news to follow.

NINE—This is a good throw. Happy events, but there might be a hint of scandal.

TEN—Uncertainty. Nothing worse. You'll just have to wait and see.

ELEVEN—There's a danger you might lose some money because of a trick. Keep a tight hold of your purse.

TWELVE—Someone wants to envolve you in a plot. Don't do any favours for people today because you might be used.

THIRTEEN—An enemy wants to cause you some trouble. Throw the dice again and if the number is higher then they won't succeed.

FOURTEEN—You are going to go on a long journey quite soon. It will be profitable but also hard work. Always be hopeful.

FIFTEEN—Some domestic trouble. Try and find out who's up to mischief then sort it out.

SIXTEEN—You're going to succeed in something which you thought was going to be a failure. But tell nobody about your success for at least a week. Sixteen also warns you to stop worrying about money, there are other more important things which you should be thinking about.

SEVENTEEN—Something very good is going to happen which will come as a complete surprise.

EIGHTEEN—This is the very best throw of all. A great future. But remember the old saying **"pride comes before a fall."**

A PROUD '18'

HERE COMES THE FALL

If you would like to receive a newsletter telling you about our new children's books, fill in the coupon with your name and address and send it to:

Gillian Osband,

Transworld Publishers Ltd,

Century House,

61–63 Uxbridge Road, Ealing,

London, W5 5SA

Name ....

Address ....

....

CHILDREN'S NEWSLETTER

All the books on the previous pages are available at your bookshop or can be ordered direct from Transworld Publishers Ltd., Cash Sales Dept. P.O. Box 11, Falmouth, Cornwall.

Please send full name and address together with cheque or postal order—no currency, and allow 40p per book to cover postage and packing (plus 18p each for additional copies).